et has a voice   Silence is a
not void   Truth can be mute
Quiet has a voice   Silence is a word   Stillnes
s not void   Truth can be mute

From Your Teachers,
Hat Stephanie,
Pre-K
Jarrod, Limor,
Crystal and Larissa.

This is a story about a
boy with a leaf growing
from his hair.

Leaf

STEPHEN MICHAEL KING'S
studio is on a windy hill
atop a coastal island.
There, with his family,
he gardens and builds wiggly walls.

He loves to draw and dream
and he's at his happiest when
an idea grows beyond his
original imagining.

Visit Stephen Michael King at
www.smkbooks.com

For Rosie and Family

Thanks to Ana Vivas, Andrew Berkhut and Margaret Connolly

A Neal Porter Book
Published by Roaring Brook Press
Roaring Brook Press is a division of Holtzbrinck Publishing Holdings Limited Partnership
175 Fifth Avenue, New York, New York 10010

www.roaringbrookpress.com
First published in Australia by Scholastic Press

Distributed in Canada by H. B. Fenn and Company, Ltd.

Cataloging-in-Publication Data is on file at the Library of Congress.
ISBN-13: 978-1-59643-503-2
ISBN-10: 1-59643-503-8

Roaring Brook Press books are available for special promotions and premiums.
For details contact: Director of Special Markets, Holtzbrinck Publishers.

Printed in China
First American edition March 2009
2 4 6 8 10 9 7 5 3 1

Leaf

Ideas, sound effects, and pictures

by

Stephen Michael King

A Neal Porter Book • Roaring Brook Press • New York

swish

Snip
snip

Snip
snip

Flap
flap
Boing
boing

Flutter
flap

Buzzzzzz

Whooooosh

Ruff
Whoosh

Wuff

Glurg
glug

Boing

Sploosh

flapper
flapper
flap

Drip
drip

Pitter
patter
Splot

z z z z Z Z Z

Snip
snap

Boing

boing

Screech

Clickity
clack

Chop
Chop
Snippity
Snip
Snip
Clack
Clackity
Choppity
Snip
Chop

Snip

t has a voice Silence is a word Stillness is not void Truth can be mute

not void Truth can be mute Quiet has a voice Silence is a word Stillness

et has a voice Silence is a word Stillness is not void Truth can be mute
Quiet has a voice Silence is a word
et has a voice Silence is a word Stillness is not void Truth can be mute Stilln